For Swee Hong
and James

*There are days when Bartholomew is naughty,
and other days when he is very very good.*

First published 1991 by Walker Books Ltd
87 Vauxhall Walk, London SE11 5HJ

This edition published 2008

Reprinted 2008, 2011

© 1991, 2007 Virginia Miller

The moral rights of the author/illustrator
have been asserted.

This book has been typeset in Garamond.

Printed in China

All rights reserved

British Library Cataloguing in Publication Data:
a catalogue record for this book is
available from the British Library.

ISBN 978-1-4063-1185-3

www.walker.co.uk

Please renew/return this item by the last date shown.
Please call the number below:

Renewals and enquiries: 0300 123 4049

Textphone for hearing or
speech impaired users: 0300 123 4041

www.hertsdirect.org/librarycatalogue

L32

ON YOUR POTTY!

Virginia Miller

WALKER BOOKS
AND SUBSIDIARIES
LONDON · BOSTON · SYDNEY · AUCKLAND

One morning George padded quietly over to Bartholomew's bed to see if he was awake.

He asked softly, "Are you awake, Ba?"

"Nah!" said Bartholomew.

George asked, "Are you up, Ba?"

"Nah!" said Bartholomew.

George asked,

"Do you need your potty, Ba?"

"Nah!" said Bartholomew.

"Nah,   nah,

nah, nah, NAH!" said Bartholomew.

"On your

potty!"

George said
in a big voice.

Bartholomew

sat on his potty.

He tried ...

and he tried …   **but nothing happened.**

"Nah!" said Bartholomew

in a little voice.

"Never mind," said George.

"Out you go and play, and be good."

"Nah!" said Bartholomew,

and off he went.

Suddenly Bartholomew thought,

On your potty!

He ran …

and he ran ...

as fast as he could …

and reached his potty …

just … in … time.

He padded proudly off to find George,

who gave him a great big hug.

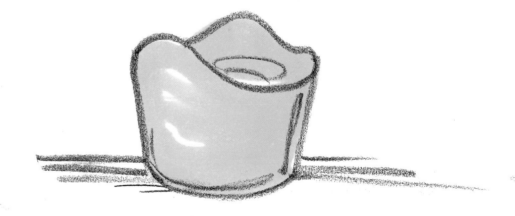